To Eric: To remind him that stories don't always end

just because they change.

by
Mildred M. Petrie
Illustrated by
Shirley Errickson

Duck-Duck

The Different Duck

*T*his might be the day," Duck-Duck said to himself
as he peeked out from under one of his small white wings.
It was very early, that magic time of neither night nor
day. Canopus was still bright in the southern sky. A sliver
of moon was fading in the west, and from the east came
a glow that was more promise than light. The air had a
color with no name. But soon the dew began to glisten,
and the little Florida lake rippled with eagerness for the
day to begin. There was not a sound.

Then from a far-away high tree came the whir of great
wings cutting silence into slices, and Duck-Duck knew
that Harold the heron was on his way. In a few minutes
the big blue-grey bird glided to his fishing place, only a
few feet from the shallow inlet where Duck-Duck lived.

"Cheer! Cheer!" whistled the cardinal.

"Everybody up! Everybody up!"

There was a faint stirring high in the treetops. In a low bush a thrush began to sing, going back again and again until his notes were practice perfect.

Little songs running up and down meant the robins were awake. And soon the mockingbirds were in full voice, imitating every sound they heard. Only the doves were sleepyheads. In soft sad tones they complained about being wakened, while blue jays screamed their scorn at anyone displeased with this beautiful morning.

Duck-Duck stretched his wings and listened. This was his favorite time of day.

"I really should go today," he said to himself firmly. "But then again," he hesitated, "maybe I should stay where it is safe for at least one more day." It wasn't exactly that he was afraid. It was just that he was a very small duck and he wasn't sure he was ready for such a big adventure.

Harold the heron was already on duty standing like a

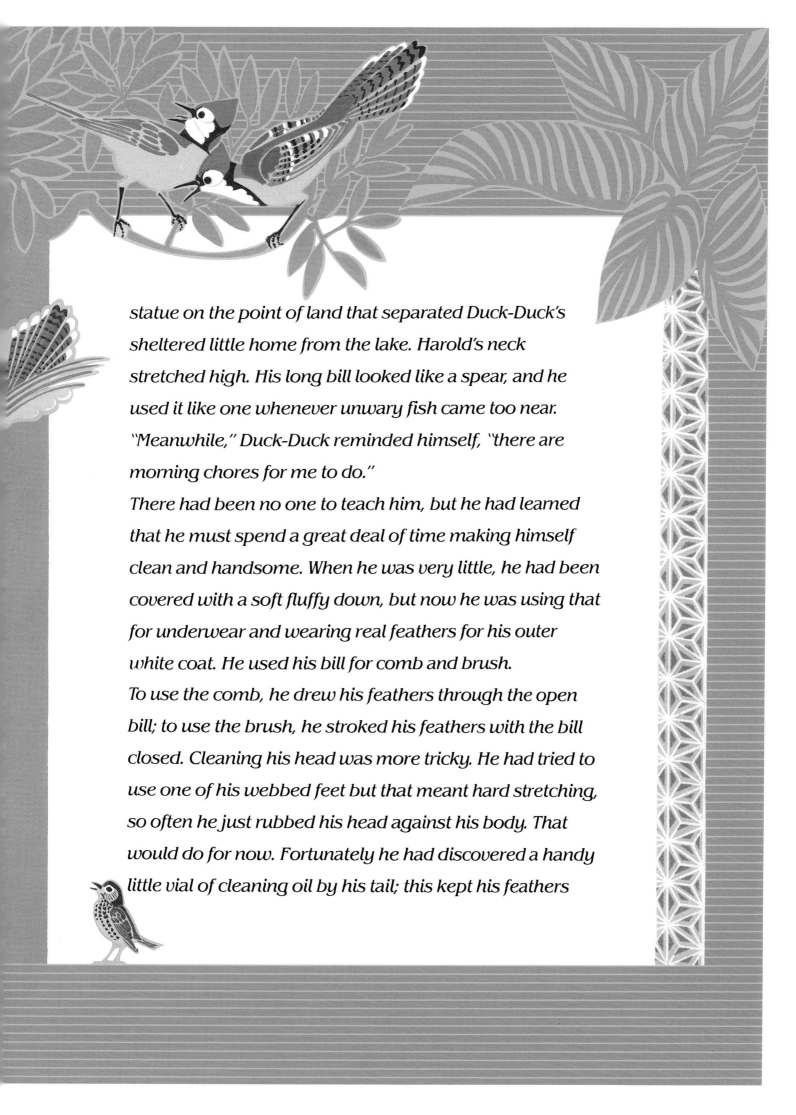

statue on the point of land that separated Duck-Duck's sheltered little home from the lake. Harold's neck stretched high. His long bill looked like a spear, and he used it like one whenever unwary fish came too near. "Meanwhile," Duck-Duck reminded himself, "there are morning chores for me to do."

There had been no one to teach him, but he had learned that he must spend a great deal of time making himself clean and handsome. When he was very little, he had been covered with a soft fluffy down, but now he was using that for underwear and wearing real feathers for his outer white coat. He used his bill for comb and brush.

To use the comb, he drew his feathers through the open bill; to use the brush, he stroked his feathers with the bill closed. Cleaning his head was more tricky. He had tried to use one of his webbed feet but that meant hard stretching, so often he just rubbed his head against his body. That would do for now. Fortunately he had discovered a handy little vial of cleaning oil by his tail; this kept his feathers soft and shining.

As long as he could remember he had been able to swim. Right after he had pecked his way through an egg shell in the pet store window and the warm air had dried his little body, he had made his way to a nearby pan of water. He had flopped in headfirst but popped back right side up. Then he had moved his tiny yellow legs and away he went, traveling on the water. What fun!

"It's even easier now," he said. "All I have to do is trust the air in all these fluffy feathers I wear."

Always after his morning swim there were morning exercises—stretch wings high, flap ten times, stretch neck up, chin in, touch chest, then stretch neck back. ("And while I'm here, I might as well comb out those back feathers a bit.") Stretch one leg, then the other. One wing out, the other out. "One! Two! One! Two!"

Neck up high then clear down to those orange-stockinged feet. A slow slide into the water for another brief swim, then out again for a roll in the grass and back to preening

and arranging those feathers again. It was a never-ending
chore, but this morning he knew he was dilly-dallying.
Next came breakfast.

Most baby ducks have mothers to show them where food
can be found, but Duck-Duck had had to learn for himself.
He tried everything in sight or in reach, pecking at seeds,
which were very, very good, even leaves. And if he
dabbled along in muddy water by the edge of the lake,
keeping his bill half underneath, a small sieve in his mouth
strained out many tasty insects. He had learned that by
tipping up his tail and reaching down to the bottom of the
shallow water he could find his juiciest meals. Could this,
he wondered, be what people called 'ducking'?

He swallowed everything whole, for he had no teeth, but
his digestion was so good it didn't matter if he gobbled a
bit. Today Duck-Duck took more time than usual. He found
a few special grasshoppers, several fish eggs, and a
curious spider that dropped   down too far from
the big oak tree where   Duck-Duck rested.

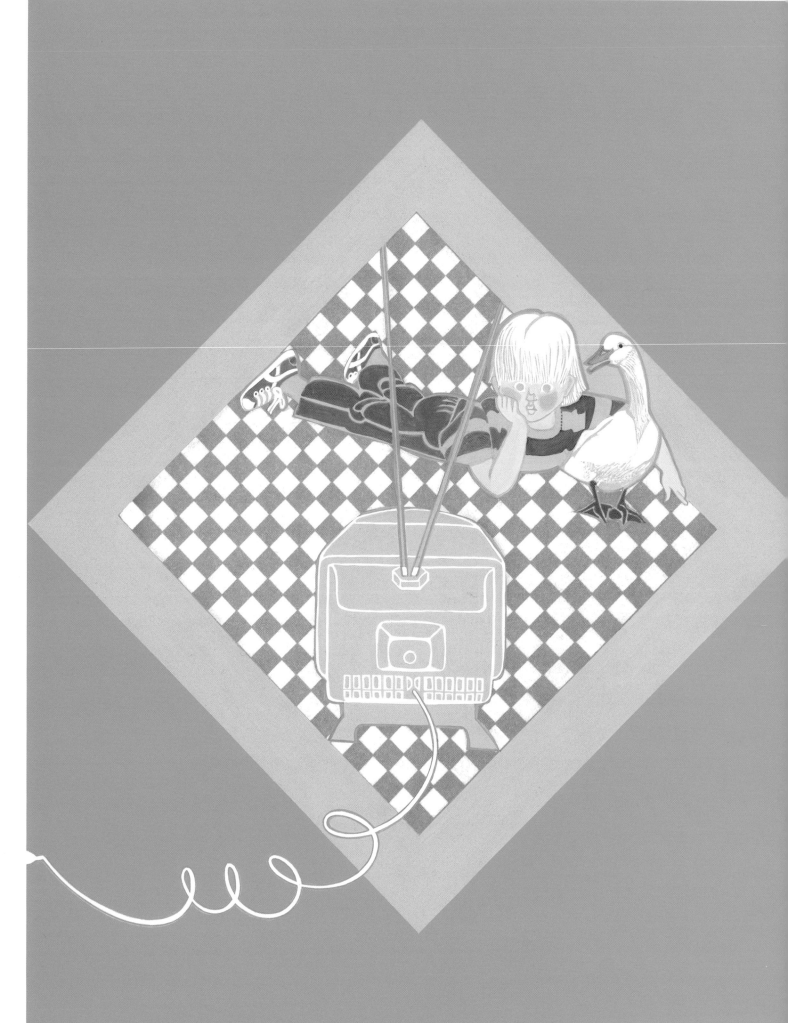

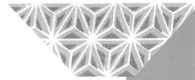

"Oh this is nice," Duck-Duck said to himself.

From around the bend and under a bridge, far at the other end of the lake, he could hear the rest of the world coming awake. "Perhaps I should go up there today," he told himself again. "Surely I'm old enough and wise enough now to make the long journey." But just when he was about to slide into the water, he heard Eric calling from the house. "Here Duck-Duck! Here Duck-Duck!"

That's how he had learned his name in the first place. When Eric's Uncle Joe placed a small lined box on the kitchen table the little boy's eyes had grown as big as they were happy, especially when a round bit of fluff looked over the edge of the box. "Duck! Duck!" said Eric.

Duck-Duck liked his name. He liked being the same coming or going, one way or the other.

At first Duck-Duck had stayed in his box in the kitchen much of the time. He splashed in a pan of water and ate cereal. Sometimes he followed Eric into the family room to watch T.V.

But one day late in spring Eric and his father and his mother walked together from the house to the edge of the little lake, where the water was shallow. Here the lake was narrow. They lifted Duck-Duck from his box and put him down in a protected cove hardly bigger than his pan of water in the kitchen. Here Duck-Duck grew and thrived and each day Eric would run down to the lake and call. "Here Duck-Duck! Here Duck-Duck!"

It was a small, small world where Duck-Duck lived, but it was safe. Harold the heron stood guard on stilts defying all intruders.

Duck-Duck had begun to suspect that he was not a people duck. Already he had learned that cereal was really not his kind of food, and he thought that somewhere out there in that noisy world far away he could find other water birds just like himself. He wanted to go where they were—not just anywhere, because that was not enough, or not everywhere, because that was too much. What he wanted more than anything in the world was to be brave enough

to go from here to there.

But not today.

Already the sun was high in the sky; he was far too sleepy for anything but a nap. Maybe tomorrow he would go. Next morning Duck-Duck woke earlier than usual, did his chores, ate his breakfast then swam farther and farther, clear out to the point where Harold stood motionless. Never before had he ventured so far. Sometimes when he had gone too near Harold, the big heron had given him a scolding glance and stalked away a few feet. But this time, Harold made it clear, Duck-Duck had gone too far.

"Squawk! Squawk!" said Harold in his hoarse voice as Duck-Duck rounded the point. "Squawk! Squawk!" he shouted again and he lifted his big wings, rested his long neck against his shoulders in a big S, and with his long legs straight back, soared far away out of sight.

Duck-Duck was so startled that he jumped straight up in the air. And wonder of wonders—he found himself flying! Flying! How wonderful!

He was so excited that he knew for certain this was the day for his big journey. He would fly a while, then settle down on the water and swim. Traveling would be no problem. "I'd better practice that landing bit first. That first flop was a hard one. This time I'll spread my tail and beat my wings hard while I use my brakes. There! I made it—much better. Just pedal backwards, then when I touch down, throw my feet forward and skid until I stop. Oh, Oh! That isn't quite as easy as I thought. I'd better swim most of the way." After what seemed like a very long time he reached the open water where the lake became wide and deep. It seemed to be forever long, blue and beautiful.

Far up the lake the morning had begun. Dozens of shapes of moving things could be seen. Climbing up on a bank in early sunshine were big black turtles; Duck-Duck shied away from that side of the lake. Already the anhingas with their long brown velvet necks had finished their swimming and fishing. Now they were roosting on swaying branches, fanning their wide black wings to dry.

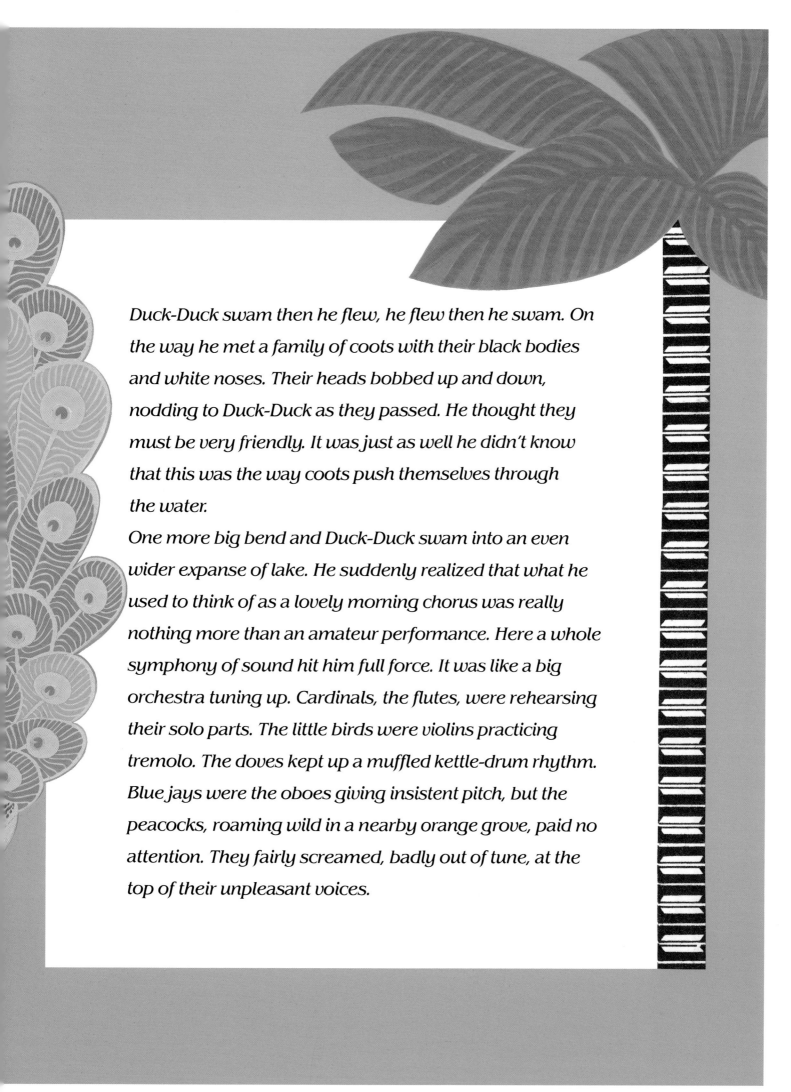

Duck-Duck swam then he flew, he flew then he swam. On the way he met a family of coots with their black bodies and white noses. Their heads bobbed up and down, nodding to Duck-Duck as they passed. He thought they must be very friendly. It was just as well he didn't know that this was the way coots push themselves through the water.

One more big bend and Duck-Duck swam into an even wider expanse of lake. He suddenly realized that what he used to think of as a lovely morning chorus was really nothing more than an amateur performance. Here a whole symphony of sound hit him full force. It was like a big orchestra tuning up. Cardinals, the flutes, were rehearsing their solo parts. The little birds were violins practicing tremolo. The doves kept up a muffled kettle-drum rhythm. Blue jays were the oboes giving insistent pitch, but the peacocks, roaming wild in a nearby orange grove, paid no attention. They fairly screamed, badly out of tune, at the top of their unpleasant voices.

"Me- Me- Me!" sang the mockingbird, then at a higher pitch, "Here I am. You can't drown me out." He was soon off in a frenzy of trying to sing his own song as well as everyone else's. Bob White, in his coat of soft brown colors, answered the roll call again and again, insisting that he be counted present. Coots with their white noses and gallinules with their red noses were the woodwind sounds.

And underneath and over all this was a new sound Duck-Duck had never heard before — "Quack! Quack!" The scene was almost more than Duck-Duck could believe. On the far shore a colony of wood storks, almost as big as Harold the heron, fished with long curved bills. In shallow water near the land the little blue and green herons were searching for breakfast. A few seagulls, tourists for the day, flew in from the nearby gulf and noisily settled down on the water. And with hoarse croaks, the grey broad-winged night herons were coming in to roost in the pine trees; they did their fishing at night.

Egrets were the other tall birds. They wore black stockings and had yellow bills. Otherwise they were as white as the snow Duck-Duck had never seen. In fact, they were as white as he was.

What interested Duck-Duck most were the dozens and dozens of creatures almost his size and shape but of different colors. Not one was white. Some were brown, others had green necks. Or was the color blue? Well, it depended on how he looked at them. They wore white necklaces and bright blue side feathers.

These were mallard ducks and he soon learned that it was the girl ducks that did all the noisy quacking. Boy ducks kept up a quiet, wheezy conversation among themselves, muttering small secrets to each other.

Some of the other ducks were bigger than Duck-Duck — the muscovies — and they wore crazy-quilt black and white coats and bright red hats. The wood ducks were the prettiest, smaller than he, and they wore squares and triangles of bright colors.

Duck-Duck was ecstatic. He had found his own kind, the family to which he must surely belong. The only difference was that he was all white, with no color at all except for his bill and his orange stockings.

He was sure this difference would make no difference.

He swam as fast as he could, then with one big leap up into the air he flew the rest of the way.

It was the longest distance he was ever to fly. It seemed that no matter how hard he flew or how fast he swam, he could never reach the other ducks. Not really. But that's the rest of the story.

With his small body almost bursting with happy anticipation he dropped with a splash into the middle of the swimming ducks. Without a glance in his direction, they simply turned and swam away from him.

What could be wrong? Well, he would try again.

He stretched his wings to dry, preened a bit to tidy himself up and decided to join them for lunch. This time they did not ignore him; they simply chased him away with a great

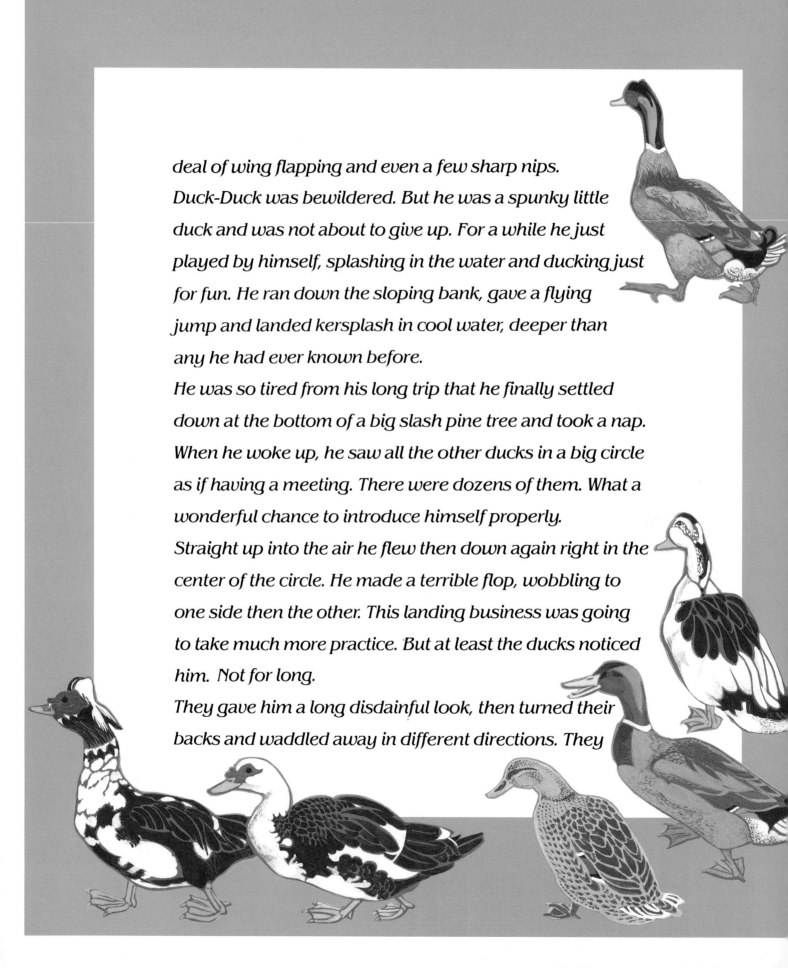

deal of wing flapping and even a few sharp nips. Duck-Duck was bewildered. But he was a spunky little duck and was not about to give up. For a while he just played by himself, splashing in the water and ducking just for fun. He ran down the sloping bank, gave a flying jump and landed kersplash in cool water, deeper than any he had ever known before.

He was so tired from his long trip that he finally settled down at the bottom of a big slash pine tree and took a nap. When he woke up, he saw all the other ducks in a big circle as if having a meeting. There were dozens of them. What a wonderful chance to introduce himself properly. Straight up into the air he flew then down again right in the center of the circle. He made a terrible flop, wobbling to one side then the other. This landing business was going to take much more practice. But at least the ducks noticed him. Not for long.

They gave him a long disdainful look, then turned their backs and waddled away in different directions. They

traveled in small groups, sometimes twos and threes,
sometimes as many as five or six. Even one that was old
and blind moved away, her friends guiding her carefully
away from Duck-Duck. They plainly did not care for his
company. Duck-Duck's feelings were very hurt.

He stayed as close as he dared the rest of the day. To tell
the truth, he sulked, and he was not a little angry. When
night came he was really scared. The other ducks swam
together far up around another big bend, but Duck-Duck
did not follow. He knew he was not wanted. He was too
tired to go home. And too sad. So he fluffed up his
napping place by the big pine tree and went to sleep.

Meanwhile Eric had run down to the little cove many
times during the day calling, "Here Duck-Duck!"

But Duck-Duck, much too far away to hear, did not come.
What Eric never knew was that early next morning, long
before he was awake, Duck-Duck slipped into the water
and glided back to the place of his beginnings. There was
Harold the heron, fishing as usual. Duck-Duck did not

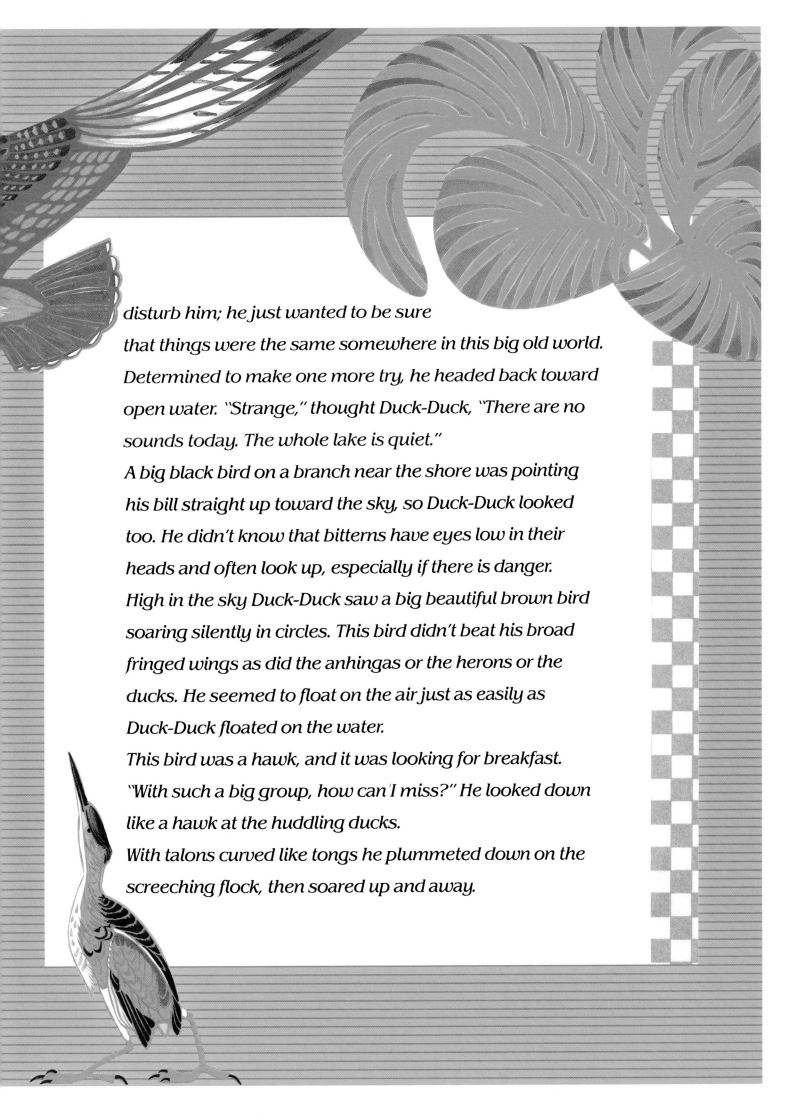

disturb him; he just wanted to be sure
that things were the same somewhere in this big old world.
Determined to make one more try, he headed back toward
open water. "Strange," thought Duck-Duck, "There are no
sounds today. The whole lake is quiet."
A big black bird on a branch near the shore was pointing
his bill straight up toward the sky, so Duck-Duck looked
too. He didn't know that bitterns have eyes low in their
heads and often look up, especially if there is danger.
High in the sky Duck-Duck saw a big beautiful brown bird
soaring silently in circles. This bird didn't beat his broad
fringed wings as did the anhingas or the herons or the
ducks. He seemed to float on the air just as easily as
Duck-Duck floated on the water.
This bird was a hawk, and it was looking for breakfast.
"With such a big group, how can I miss?" He looked down
like a hawk at the huddling ducks.
With talons curved like tongs he plummeted down on the
screeching flock, then soared up and away.

On the ground lay a dead mallard, its beautiful blue-green feathers scattered in all directions.

Again the big brown hawk swooped down. This time he used the sharp hook of his bill and began his feast.

"Strange," again thought Duck-Duck. "The ducks don't act frightened any more."

They were paying little attention to the hawk as he ate, going about their usual business of the day—searching for food, tidying up, bathing—as if they understood this was nature's way. The hawk, they seemed to know, wouldn't attack again that day. There was food and food enough; he would not kill unnecessarily. But all day Duck-Duck stayed close to his big pine tree. He was taking no chances.

"This new world seems to have many unfriendly and even dangerous creatures. But I am a lucky duck," he kept telling himself. "If I had been with the other ducks when the hawk swooped down, I might have been the one that was caught. One thing certain, there are times when it is good to be alone."

So the days came and went with Duck-Duck trying to learn how to be alone without being lonesome. Just to find food every day and to keep himself white and beautiful took many hours a day. He watched the other ducks playing and squabbling, pushing, shoving, diving, and of course, ducking. He imitated them and invented games of his own. Sometimes he was a show-off, trying to attract their attention. He found he could move much faster than they did if he flapped his wings and at the same time ran down the slope into the water. Then he would skip along the surface half flying, half swimming. That was fun too and very spectacular. On cool mornings he sometimes swam round and round in patches of sunshine until he was almost dizzy.

In late summer Duck-Duck began to lose his white feathers.

"Good," he thought, "Now maybe I'll be the same color as the others."

He lost so many feathers he couldn't even fly. He didn't

worry too much about it because all the other ducks were having the same problem. He had no way of knowing that this was 'molting', that it happened every year. After about a month new flight feathers grew in place of the old ones. This was nature's way, he guessed, and it was pleasant to have new clothes to wear each season. Even if they were white.

Duck-Duck had to learn everything for himself. The other ducks chattered away among themselves, showing each other where the best food could be found, telling of dangers and sharing the everyday news of the lake. But Duck-Duck was never allowed to listen.

It would be nice to say he finally made friends.

But he didn't.

He was different, and they would not accept him.

Come nighttime, Duck-Duck would settle down in his spot by the big pine tree. He looked like a soft white blur in the moonlight and often the lights from a house across the water surrounded him as he went to sleep. He sometimes

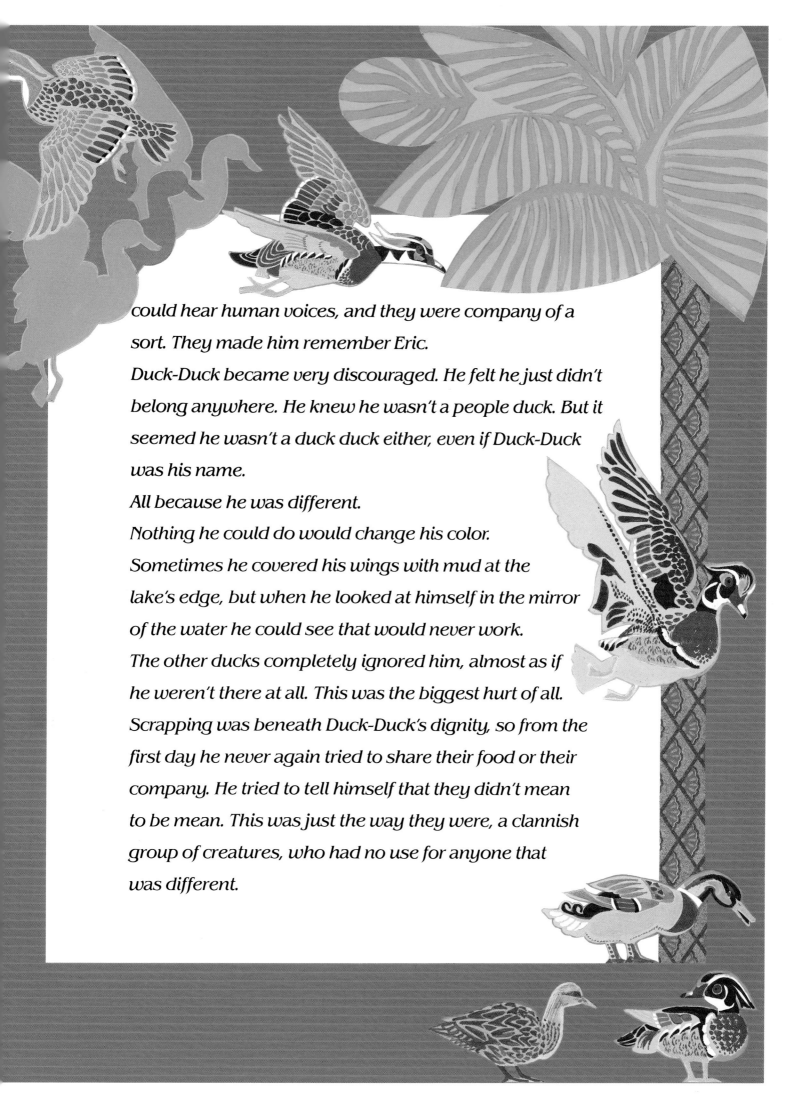

could hear human voices, and they were company of a sort. They made him remember Eric.

Duck-Duck became very discouraged. He felt he just didn't belong anywhere. He knew he wasn't a people duck. But it seemed he wasn't a duck duck either, even if Duck-Duck was his name.

All because he was different.

Nothing he could do would change his color. Sometimes he covered his wings with mud at the lake's edge, but when he looked at himself in the mirror of the water he could see that would never work.

The other ducks completely ignored him, almost as if he weren't there at all. This was the biggest hurt of all. Scrapping was beneath Duck-Duck's dignity, so from the first day he never again tried to share their food or their company. He tried to tell himself that they didn't mean to be mean. This was just the way they were, a clannish group of creatures, who had no use for anyone that was different.

This was the way their fathers and mothers and grandfathers and grandmothers had always been and they weren't about to change.

One evening, after the ducks had all gone to bed and Duck-Duck had smoothed his wings and settled down alone, who should come stalking along but Harold the heron. Like a big boy allowed out after supper, he was out for a late snack. "Move over," he squawked to Duck-Duck. If he had known how, Duck-Duck would have laughed. Here was Harold invading his territory! Now that Duck-Duck was so grown up, Harold didn't recognize him as the little white thing that had so annoyed him many months ago.

Just for old time's sake, Duck-Duck stepped aside while Harold stood and fished. As usual, Harold stood much longer than he fished — standing still was what a heron seemed to do best — then with a mighty lift of wings he soared away for the night and Duck-Duck was left in the one small place he had chosen for his own kingdom.

Here nothing else ever disturbed him again. That is, nothing until the night he was scared almost out of his wits.

In late fall a great gloom had settled over the lake. Even the morning music was more quiet. The ducks had stopped swimming. Why, Duck-Duck did not know.

Sometimes, just before time for him to go to sleep, Duck-Duck had seen what looked like an old log drifting down the lake and he wondered why it didn't stay lodged in the tangle of bushes at shoreline. But one evening he heard people talking about alligators.

"There he is!" shouted one man. "Call the wildlife officer. Alligators are dangerous to children and pets, and I believe they are eating our crop of water babies this year."

"Yes," said his neighbor. "Did you know they can move very fast if they are angry? When they sweep those big strong tails back and forth in the water, they are also very fast swimmers."

"Nothing," said the first man, "is safe from a hungry

alligator—herons, raccoons, certainly ducks. It will eat anything it can swallow and it has the teeth for taking big bites."

"DUCKS!" Duck-Duck shuddered. "I must be very careful," he told himself, "and I must be very quiet." Afterward Duck-Duck held his breath each time the big log that was really an alligator glided past his tree. Sometimes during the daytime the big animal would crawl up on the opposite bank to stretch, but he did not come near Duck-Duck. More and more often, however, the stillness of the nights was torn apart by shrill distress calls as the big ducks were attacked. This was real trouble time for ducks. Duck-Duck was relieved when the wildlife officer finally arrived but was horrified to see the man tie a long rope around Duck-Duck's own tree. He also tied the rope to a stick that extended over the water, and on the end of that stick was a hook with alligator bait.

"Alligator bait!" thought Duck-Duck. "That could be me if I'm not very careful."

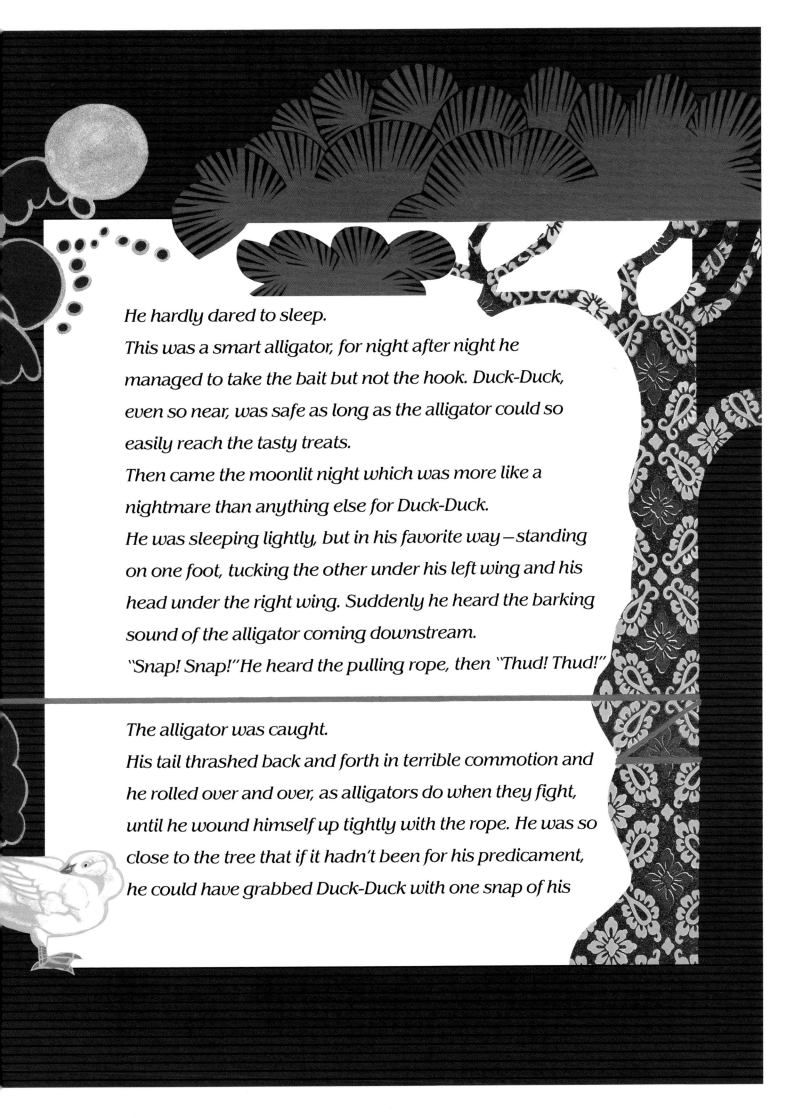

He hardly dared to sleep.

This was a smart alligator, for night after night he managed to take the bait but not the hook. Duck-Duck, even so near, was safe as long as the alligator could so easily reach the tasty treats.

Then came the moonlit night which was more like a nightmare than anything else for Duck-Duck.

He was sleeping lightly, but in his favorite way—standing on one foot, tucking the other under his left wing and his head under the right wing. Suddenly he heard the barking sound of the alligator coming downstream.

"Snap! Snap!" He heard the pulling rope, then "Thud! Thud!"

The alligator was caught.

His tail thrashed back and forth in terrible commotion and he rolled over and over, as alligators do when they fight, until he wound himself up tightly with the rope. He was so close to the tree that if it hadn't been for his predicament, he could have grabbed Duck-Duck with one snap of his

great jaws. His eyes shone in the dark like round red
rubies and his big strong cone-shaped teeth seemed to
have no end of counting. He made loud hissing noises.
When he blew out his breath the sound was like thunder.
"Alligators," the man had said, "have more strength to
close their mouths than to open them, one advantage they
have over people."

Luckily for Duck-Duck, this alligator's mouth was full, and
busy, and closed.

All night long the fury went on. Duck-Duck had trained
himself to be very quiet whenever the alligator was near;
now he couldn't have moved if he had tried, he was
that scared.

Early the next morning the wildlife officer was pleased to
see his catch. He dragged the angry alligator up on the
bank, made sure its mouth was securely roped, cut the
rope from around Duck-Duck's tree, flipped the alligator
over on his back, and ran a finger down its tummy.
Instantly the furious creature became still.

"Nobody knows why that works," said the officer. "But it always does. He'll swallow the hook now and it will never hurt him. I'll take him out to the State Park area. That's where alligators are just as protected from people as people here in the suburbs are protected from alligators." With a big heave he tossed the animal into his truck and drove away.

Duck-Duck felt like a hero.

It had been his tree that had caught the alligator and thereby protected the whole neighborhood.

Of course no one knew it, he didn't suppose. The other ducks paid no attention to him as usual, as indifferent as always. But he didn't much care.

With even more care than usual, Duck-Duck preened his white feathers and slid into the water. This was a very special day for him, and he would celebrate by going back to where he began. How he wished that he could tell Eric the scarey story.

It was much too early for Eric to be awake. But Harold the

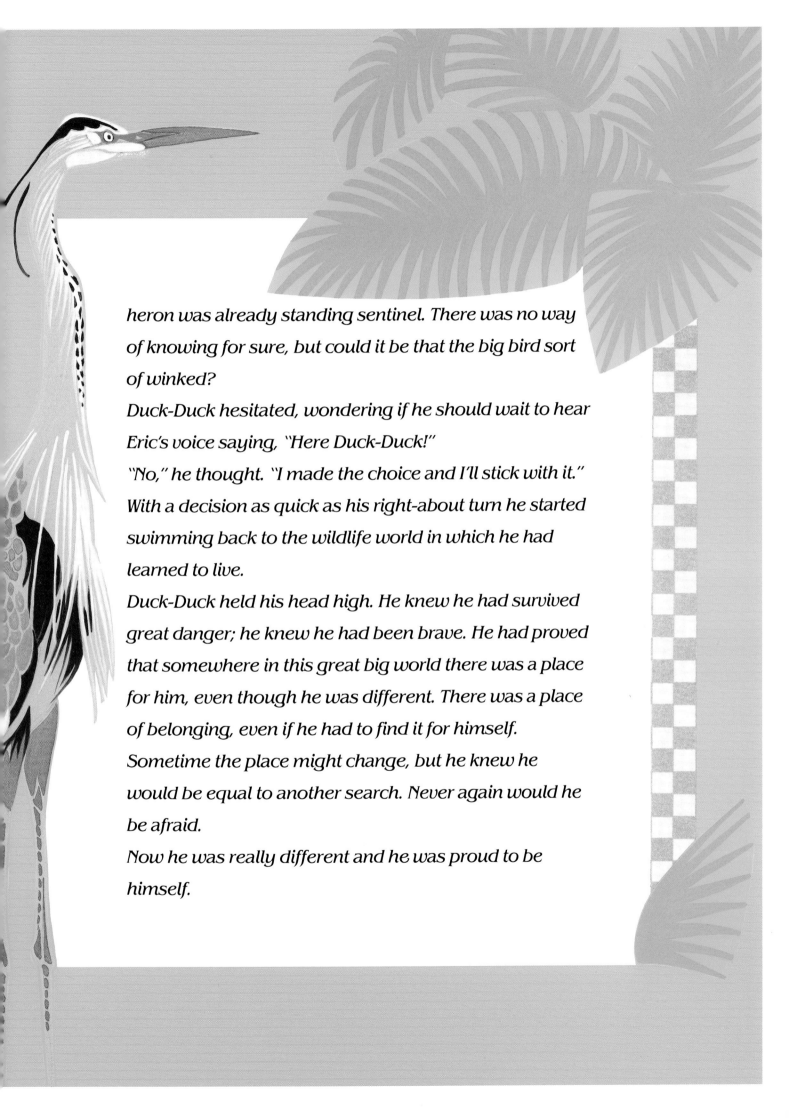

heron was already standing sentinel. There was no way of knowing for sure, but could it be that the big bird sort of winked?

Duck-Duck hesitated, wondering if he should wait to hear Eric's voice saying, "Here Duck-Duck!"

"No," he thought. "I made the choice and I'll stick with it." With a decision as quick as his right-about turn he started swimming back to the wildlife world in which he had learned to live.

Duck-Duck held his head high. He knew he had survived great danger; he knew he had been brave. He had proved that somewhere in this great big world there was a place for him, even though he was different. There was a place of belonging, even if he had to find it for himself. Sometime the place might change, but he knew he would be equal to another search. Never again would he be afraid.

Now he was really different and he was proud to be himself.

Distributed by the Florida Literary Foundation, Inc.
2516 Ridge Avenue, Sarasota FL 34235

ISBN 1-877978-41-8
Library of Congress Card Catalogue No. 87-80921

Manufactured in the United States of America
All rights reserved.